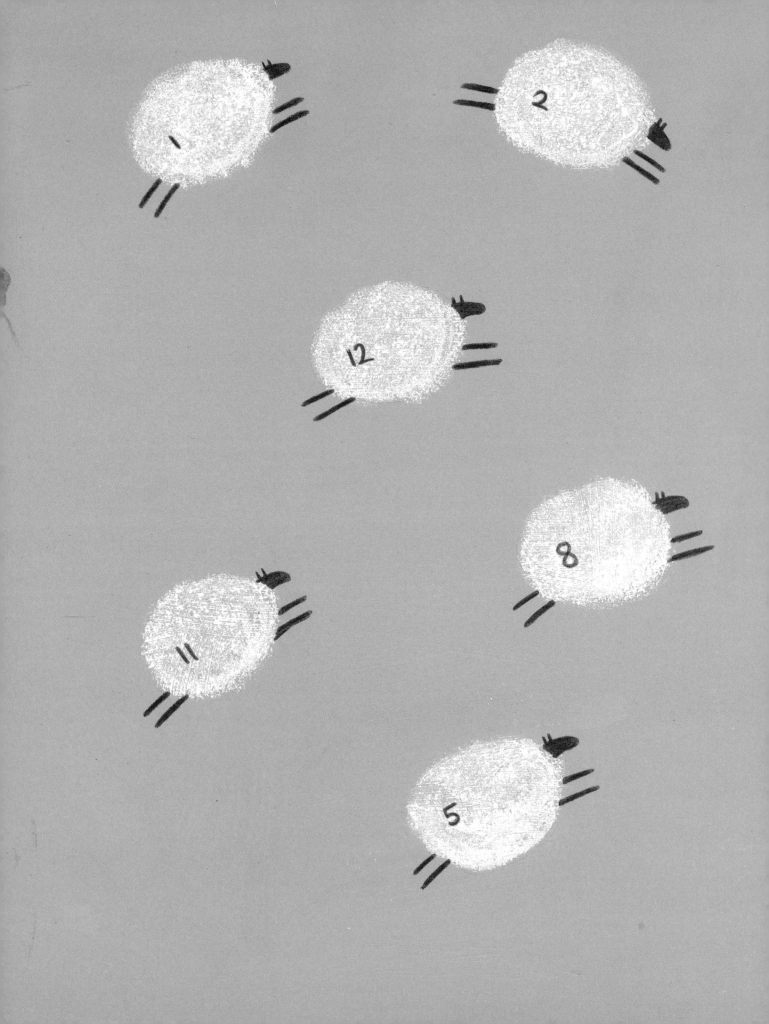

THE PRINCE'S BEDTIME

To Stephanie and her prince charming, David.
Happy 20th! Love, Mom — J. O.

Dedicated with love and kisses to Seb,
my lovely husband — M. L.

Barefoot Books, 2067 Massachusetts Ave, Cambridge, MA 02140

Text copyright © 2006 by Joanne Oppenheim
Illustrations copyright © 2006 by Miriam Latimer
The moral right of Joanne Oppenheim to be identified as the author and
Miriam Latimer to be identified as the illustrator of this work
has been asserted

This book was typeset in
Fontesque Bold 24 on 33 point
The illustrations were
prepared in acrylics
and collage

Graphic design by Judy Linard, London
Color separation by Grafiscan, Verona
Printed and bound in Singapore by Tien Wah Press Pte Ltd

This book has been printed on 100% acid-free paper

Library of Congress Cataloging-in-Publication Data
Oppenheim, Joanne.
 The Prince's bedtime / written by Joanne Oppenheim ;
illustrated by Miriam Latimer.
   p. cm.
 Summary: When the Prince refuses to go to bed each night,
people come from near and far with "cures," but an old woman
knows the best way of putting children to sleep.
 ISBN 1-84148-597-7 (hardcover : alk. paper)
 [1. Princes--Fiction. 2. Bedtime--Fiction. 3. Books and
reading--Fiction. 4. Stories in rhyme.] I. Latimer, Miriam, ill.
II. Title.
 PZ8.3.O615Pr 2005
 [E]--dc22
              2004028593

         1 3 5 7 9 8 6 4 2

THE PRINCE'S BEDTIME

Written by
Joanne Oppenheim
Illustrated by
Miriam Latimer

Barefoot Books
Celebrating Art and Story

In a faraway kingdom, a long time ago,
When bedtime drew near, the Prince shouted, "No!"

The Queen tucked her son in a quilt made of silk.
The cook brought him cookies. The maid brought hot milk.

Though everyone tried hard to make the Prince sleep,
The harder they tried, the more he would weep.

"This cannot go on," said the King. "I am sure
That somebody somewhere knows some sort of cure!

So the next day he sent forth a royal request
To the north, to the south, to the east and the west:

"IF ANYONE KNOWS HOW
TO MAKE THE PRINCE REST,
PLEASE COME AT ONCE
TO THE ROYAL ADDRESS!"

The first to arrive was a bearded physician
Who promised his medicine would cure the condition.

The Prince closed his lips as tight as could be.
"It's good," said his mother. "Just taste it and see."

But the Prince shook his head and pulled up the cover.
The doctor said, "Watch, I'll give some to your mother."

The Queen took a spoonful: "M-m-m," she said sweetly.
"Delicious!" She yawned, and was instantly sleepy.

The courtiers then followed their queen's fine example.
They each took one sip, and that one sip was ample.

They all licked their lips: "M-m-m, it's so sweet!"
Then, quick as a wink, they all fell asleep . . .

Except for the Prince, who heard them all snoring
And said with disgust, "How perfectly boring!"

The next night five dancers
arrived with musicians.
"We'll dance 'til he's tired –
come, take your positions."

The signal was given, the dancers began.
Some say they danced, but really they ran

Around in a circle, first left and then right.
They whirled and they twirled well into the night.

They danced through the castle 'til quarter past four,
When the King cried, "Enough! My feet are too sore!"

Then all of them groaned and collapsed on the floor,
Except for the Prince, who begged, "Let's dance some more!"

The next to arrive at the old castle gate
Was a mustached magician in high hat and cape.

"Your Grace," he announced, "with your kind permission,
My hypnotic spells can cure this condition."

"Proceed," the King yawned. "Do what you can."
"I'll start with some tricks," the magician began.

With a wave of his hand and a whisper of words
He brought forth from nowhere a flurry of birds,

A bouquet of roses, a rabbit of course,
And last but not least, he brought forth a horse!

"A HORSE IN THE CASTLE!"

the Queen screamed. "NO MORE!"

"Guards!" called the King, "Show him the door!"
"Oh, why?" the Prince cried, "Can't I have a ride?"

The next night at bedtime the Prince got a present.
A feather-down quilt stuffed with feathers of pheasant.

"Sire," said the peasant who brought him the present,
"The Prince cannot sleep in a bed that's unpleasant.

Try this, little boy, it's as soft as new snow.
You'll drift off to dreamland. You'll love it, I know."

The Prince was so happy he jumped in headfirst.
He jumped in so hard that the feather quilt burst.

"ACHOO!" wheezed the King. "ACHOO!" sneezed the Queen
It took them all morning to get the place clean.

But the Prince was so tickled
he giggled all night:
He laughed and he laughed
at the ludicrous sight.

Night after night they tried to amuse him.
Night after night there was endless confusion.

Jugglers tried juggling. Jesters made gestures.
Learned professors made countless conjectures.

Nurse sang a lullaby. Cook baked a cake.
But alas the small Prince still stayed wide awake.

Then one windy night (it was long after eight)
An old woman came to the great palace gate.

"Your Majesties, please –" she curtsied quite low.
"I'll get him to sleep if you'll just stop this show."

"And what do you do? Do you dance? Can you sing?
What's in your bag? What did you bring?"

"Of course I can dance, and I do love to sing.
But for bedtime," she said, "I've the very best thing."

Reaching into her basket she pulled out a book,
And said to the Prince, "I'll read while you look."

"But where are the pictures?" he asked in surprise.
"You'll see them," she said, "if you just close your eyes."

So that's what he did. He shut his eyes tight.
And soon after that . . .

. . . fell asleep for the night.

Barefoot Books
Celebrating Art and Story

At Barefoot Books, we celebrate art and story that opens
the hearts and minds of children from all walks of life, inspiring
them to read deeper, search further, and explore their own creative gifts.
Taking our inspiration from many different cultures, we focus on themes that
encourage independence of spirit, enthusiasm for learning, and sharing of
the world's diversity. Interactive, playful and beautiful, our products
combine the best of the present with the best of the past to
educate our children as the caretakers of tomorrow.

www.barefootbooks.com